# Tatum and Her TIGER

Autumn House® Publishing
www.autumnhousepublishing.com
A Division of **REVIEW AND HERALD® PUBLISHING**
Since 1861

Published by Autumn House® Publishing, a division of Review and Herald® Publishing, Hagerstown, MD 21741-1119

Autumn House® titles may be purchased in bulk for educational, business, fund-raising, or sales promotional use. For information, please e-mail: SpecialMarkets@reviewandherald.com.

Autumn House® Publishing publishes biblically-based materials for spiritual, physical, and mental growth and Christian discipleship.

The author assumes full responsibility for the accuracy of all facts and quotations as cited in this book.

This book was
Edited by Jeannette R. Johnson
Designed by Ron J. Pride
Illustrations by Andrei Vieira
Typeset: Sasoon Primary 16/20

PRINTED IN THAILAND

12  11  10  09  08                                        5  4  3  2  1

Library of Congress Cataloging-in-Publication Data

Nash, Andy, 1971-
    Tatum and her tiger : for kids blessed with passion / Andy Nash.
        p. cm.
    "Character Series (Book 1)."
    Summary: Tatum is so excited about the big spring picnic in Animaland until she and her pet, Passion, fall during the gunnysack race, but Grandpa knows how she feels and shares a special secret that lifts her spirits.
    [1. Pets—Juvenile Works. 2. Picnicking-- Juvenile Works. 3. Self-perception-- Juvenile Works. 4. Friendship-- Juvenile Works.]
I. Title. II. Title: For kids blessed with passion.
    PZ7.N1659Tat 2007
    [E]--dc22
            ISBN 978-0-8127-0451-8              2006102814

To order, call **1-800-765-6955**.
Visit us at **www.AutumnHousePublishing.com** for information on other Autumn House® products.

THIS BOOK BELONGS TO:

# MORE FROM ANDY NASH:

*Tatum and Her Tiger:* For Kids Blessed With Passion

. . . . . . . . . . . . . . . . .

**Marcus and His Monkey:** For Kids Blessed With Popularity

. . . . . . . . . . . . . . . . .

**Melinda and Her Mule:** For Kids Blessed With a Strong Will

. . . . . . . . . . . . . . . . .

**Hal and His Husky:** For Kids Blessed With Courage

. . . . . . . . . . . . . . . . .

**Hank and His Hyena:** For Kids Blessed With Humor

. . . . . . . . . . . . . . . . .

**Dave and His Doves:** For Kids Blessed With Gentleness

# DEAR GROWN-UP:

**T**he children in your life are fearfully and wonderfully made—each blessed with special characteristics!

**Learning to Bee-Me:** The Character Series is a fun yet meaningful way for your child to learn about the strengths and weaknesses of the human character—whether their own or others'. In these stories, the children each have a little sidekick, a tag-along animal that represents a child's major trait. Of course, grown-ups have these same traits, and you'll often see a child learning from a grown-up with the same "animal" in their life.

I invite you to talk about these stories with your children. Help them to identify their own "characters"—and those of others. As we learn about each other, we can better appreciate the special way we've each been made—and how much we truly need each other.

Andy Nash

# Tatum couldn't believe it.
## She could hardly stand it.
### The big day had finally arrived!

For weeks Tatum had been looking forward to the spring picnic in Animaland! Her tiger, Passion, was just as excited as Tatum was!

Tatum had been a huge help in planning the picnic.

She helped put up the big red and white tent. She helped dip the apples in caramel. (It was hard not to eat one!) She even helped come up with game ideas. "How about a gunny sack race?" she suggested.

8

"That's a great idea, Tatum," said
Miss Morgan, the woman in charge
of the picnic.

Tatum felt so happy. So did her
tiger, Passion.

9

Tatum had told everyone she knew about the big picnic.

She called her grandparents on her mom's cell phone.

"That sounds wonderful, Tatum," said her grandma. "Grandpa and I will be sure to come!"

11

At school, Tatum had told all her classmates about the picnic. "It's going to be so much fun," she said. "We're even doing gunny sack races."

But some of the kids didn't act very excited about the picnic.

"It sounds boring," said Barry. This made Tatum feel upset. Her tiger began to growl. "Calm down, Passion," she said.

When Tatum and her family arrived at the picnic, she felt excited again.

Everyone was having such a great time. People were laughing and playing and eating!

"Hey, Tatum," said a friendly boy named Marcus. "Come play with us!"

Before long a voice came over the big speaker.
"OK, everyone! It's time for the gunny sack races!
Please come to the starting line."

Tatum and her tiger raced to the starting line with the other kids.
"Here's your gunny sack," said Miss Morgan. "Have fun, Tatum."

Tatum and her tiger climbed
into their gunny sack.

Tatum looked down the line at the other kids.

There was Marcus and Hal and Melinda and Anna Grace. Even Barry was there!

Oh, boy, thought Tatum, I hope I beat Barry real good. He didn't even want to race.

All the kids and their animals leaned forward.
"On your marks. . ." said the announcer, "Get set . . . **GO!**"

19

As the cheers echoed through the trees,
Tatum and her tiger got a huge jump on the pack.
They jumped and jumped, just as they had
practiced at home in their pillowcases.
"Come on, Passion!" yelled Tatum. "Keep jumping!"

The other kids were jumping fast, too, but Tatum and her tiger were still in the lead. Just then Tatum saw a frightened pocket gopher run out of its hole.

"Passion!" she yelled. "Look out for that gopher hole—!"

21

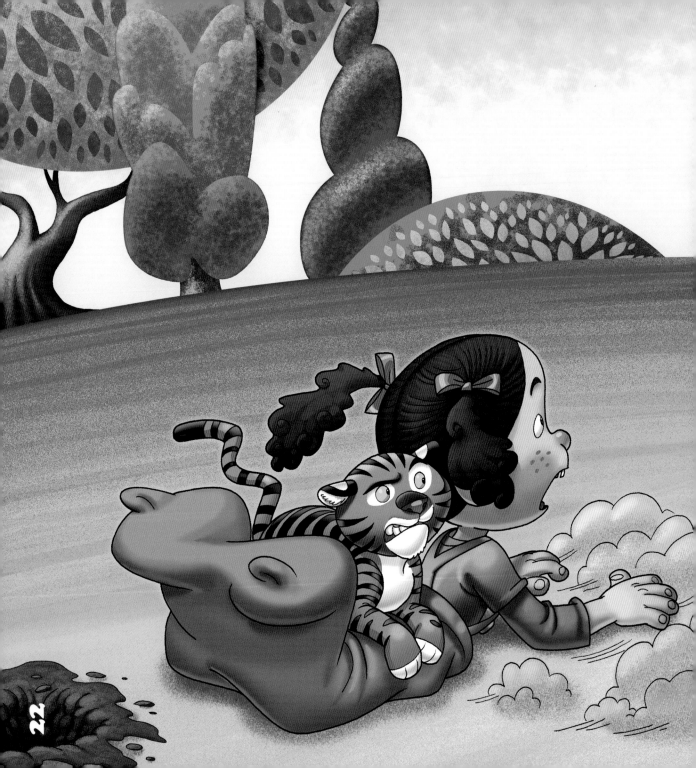

**OOOMPH!** *Tatum and Passion felt* their knees buckle under them. They were falling!

As her elbows skidded in the grass, Tatum could see the other kids bouncing past them.

It was a terrible feeling! Tatum's tiger roared angrily at the other animals.

Barry and his basset hound won first place in the gunny sack race.

**W**hen it was time to give Barry his trophy, Tatum didn't want to watch.

But someone was watching her. It was Grandpa.

"Tatum," said Grandpa. "Can I talk with you a minute?"

"OK," Tatum said quietly.

"I can see you're feeling bad," he said.

"Barry didn't even want to do gunny sacks," Tatum blurted out, crying. "He didn't even help with the picnic."

"I know," said Grandpa. "And do you know why?"

"Because he's mean," said Tatum.

"No," said Grandpa. "Because he's different."

"We're all different," explained Grandpa. "We all have different characters. That's the way we were made. We have to learn how our characters work."

"What do you mean?" Tatum asked.

"**Y**ou're a very passionate person, Tatum. People with passion feel things very deep in their heart. Your passion means that you get very excited about things. And this excitement helps others get excited."

Grandpa continued.

"But your passion also means that you feel hurt when your plans don't work out. Do you know how I know this?"

"How?" asked Tatum.

"Because I have a tiger too."

Tatum was quiet for a moment. Then she started laughing. Then they both started laughing. They laughed so hard that they almost rolled down the hill.

"Passionate
people like us
sometimes roar a
little too loud,
don't we?"
said Grandpa.

"Yeah," said Tatum.

"And when we do
that, we need to
make things right again."

"Yeah," said Tatum, looking over toward Barry.

29

**"H**ey, Barry," said Tatum. "You did really great in the race today.
"Thank you, Tatum," said Barry, smiling. "I couldn't have done it
without you."
"You mean because I fell down?" asked Tatum.
"No; because you invited me to the picnic.
I've never come to the picnic before.
But when you got so excited,
I secretly got excited too."